Jessica
the Jazz Fairy

by Daisy Meadows

Join the **Rainbow Magic Reading Challenge!**

Read the story and collect your fairy points to climb the Reading Rainbow at the back of the book.

This book is worth 5 points.

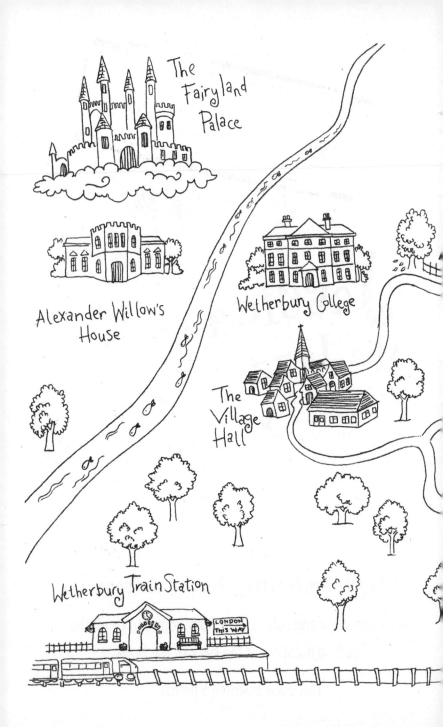

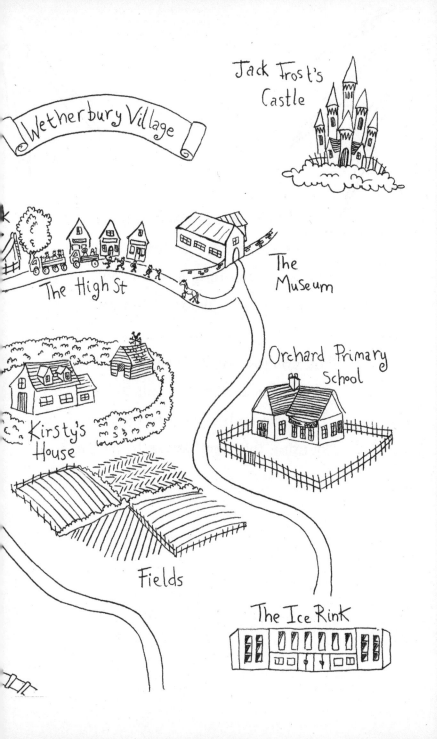

Jack Frost's Castle

Wetherbury Village

The High St

The Museum

Orchard Primary School

Kirsty's House

Fields

The Ice Rink

Hold tight to the ribbons, please.
You goblins now may feel a breeze.
I'm summoning a hurricane
To take the ribbons away again.

But, goblins, you'll be swept up too,
For I have work for you to do.
Guard each ribbon carefully,
By using this new power to freeze.

Contents

Jessica Makes an Entrance

"I'm so-o-o excited!" Kirsty Tate said
happily, smoothing down the satiny skirt
of her long purple dress. "I've never been
to a really *grown-up* party before!"

"Me neither," Rachel Walker, Kirsty's
best friend, agreed. Like Kirsty, she was
dressed in one of her favourite outfits,
a floaty ivory-coloured dress with sequins

around the hem and neckline. Along with Kirsty's parents, the girls were on their way to a party at the home of Alexander Willow, who was a friend of Mr and Mrs Tate's.

"It's not far now," Mr Tate replied, steering the car down the narrow, dark country lane. "You're going to have a great time, girls. Alexander's a producer of West End musicals, and he always throws *fantastic* parties!"

"Yes, there's going to be a jazz band and lots of dancing!" added Mrs Tate.

In the back of the car, Kirsty and Rachel exchanged an anxious glance. While Rachel was staying with Kirsty over the half-term holiday, the two girls  had been helping their very special friends, the Dance Fairies, find their missing magic Dance Ribbons. The ribbons were very important because their magic made sure that all kinds of dancing were fun, in both Fairyland and the human world, and also that dance performances went well. Jack Frost had stolen the ribbons for himself because he wanted their magic powers to help his goblins learn to dance.

When the King and Queen of Fairyland had demanded that the ribbons be returned to the Dance Fairies, Jack Frost's icy spell had sent seven of his goblin servants tumbling away into the human world, each goblin clutching one of the magic ribbons. The goblins were supposed to keep the ribbons hidden, but so far Kirsty and Rachel, with the help of the Dance Fairies, had managed to get four of them back.

"Jessica the Jazz Fairy's ribbon is still missing," Kirsty whispered eagerly. "Maybe the goblin who has her ribbon will be at the party tonight!"

Rachel nodded. The girls knew that the magical ribbon was attracted to its own type of dance. "I hope so too, Kirsty," Rachel whispered. "We must get the ribbon back otherwise the party will be ruined!"

"What kind of dancing will there be, Mum?" Kirsty asked as Mr Tate drove between two wrought iron gates and up a long, winding driveway. "Rachel and I don't really know what jazz dance is!"

Mrs Tate nodded. "Jazz music is quite modern, and so is jazz dance," she explained. "In fact, you've probably both seen lots of jazz dancing in musicals."

"Oh, great!" Rachel exclaimed happily, "I *love* that kind of dancing!"

13

Kirsty was peering out of the car window, her eyes wide. "I've never seen such an *enormous* garden!" she said. "Rachel, look at that pond with the mermaid fountain in the middle."

Rachel looked out of the window. "And *look* at the house!" she added, pointing.

The manor house in front of them was huge and very impressive with lots of windows and a large wooden door that

stood ajar, flanked by flaming torches.
Rows of cars were already parked
outside, and people were climbing out of
them. The women were dressed in long,
elegant ballgowns in a rainbow of
colours and the men all wore smart suits.

As they entered the hall of the manor
house, the girls looked around eagerly.
The house was lit by tall, pillar-shaped
white candles whose flickering flames
filled the hall with a warm yellow glow.

Golden chocolate coins had been scattered over the antique tables and large gold platters piled high with bejewelled cupcakes had been placed here and there.

"Oh, this is *gorgeous!*" Kirsty sighed.

Everyone else was making their way through the house towards the back garden, so the Tates and Rachel followed.

The garden was even more
spectacular than the house.
Kirsty and Rachel stared
open-mouthed as they
walked past exotic
plants in huge
china pots,
a rippling
aquamarine
swimming pool
and an
intricate maze
constructed of
neatly-clipped
hedges.
A white
marquee had been
erected in the middle of
the garden for the party.

As the girls walked in, they could see
that gold sparkling stars decorated the
roof of the marquee, and tables and
chairs had been set up for the guests.
A jazz band sat on a platform at the
back, playing a catchy tune that quickly
had Kirsty and Rachel tapping their toes.

"Nobody's dancing yet, thank
goodness!" Rachel whispered, noting
the empty dance floor in the middle

18

of the marquee.

"Everyone's too busy eating and talking," Kirsty whispered back, watching the waiters who were carrying around trays of drinks and offering them to the guests. "But there are lots of places for a goblin to hide!"

Rachel nodded. "We'll just have to keep looking," she said determinedly, scanning the marquee.

19

"That's Alexander over there, girls," said Mrs Tate, pointing to a tall, fair-haired man who was chatting with other guests. "We'll introduce you later, but I can tell you're longing to explore. Why don't you go and have a look around now?"

"Thanks, Mum," Kirsty said. And she and Rachel wandered off, winding their way between the chairs and tables.

"Would you like a fruit juice cocktail, girls?" asked a waiter. He was holding a tray on which stood two tall crystal glasses decorated with pretty paper umbrellas. "They're delicious."

"Yes, please!" Kirsty and Rachel chorused, each taking one of the glasses.

Rachel took a sip. "Yum!" she exclaimed as the waiter hurried off. "It *is* delicious!"

Kirsty raised the glass to her lips to take a sip herself. But then she gasped aloud, because, there, sitting on the rim of the crystal glass, twirling the umbrella and smiling up at her, was Jessica the Jazz Fairy.

Enter the Goblin

"Rachel, look!" Kirsty laughed as
Jessica rose to her feet, still holding the
umbrella. Balancing daintily on the
edge of the glass, the tiny fairy waved
up at the girls. She wore a silky pink
dress with a deeper pink sash and
a matching long, pink feather boa
around her neck. High-heeled silver

shoes sparkled on her feet, and golden
curls tumbled down her back.

"Hello, girls," Jessica called softly,
putting down the umbrella. "I've come
to find my ribbon!"

Quickly Kirsty and Rachel hurried
over to a quiet corner of the marquee

away from the other
guests. Jessica took
a cautious look around
and then fluttered
from the glass onto
Kirsty's shoulder.
"Is your ribbon here,

Jessica?" Rachel asked eagerly.

Jessica nodded. "I'm sure it is!" she
replied. "The magic of my ribbon will
have brought the goblin here because
the party has a jazz theme!"

"Ladies and gentlemen!" came a loud announcement from the stage, making Rachel and Kirsty jump.

The girls turned to see what was going on. The saxophone player from the jazz band had stepped up to the microphone and was beaming at the audience.

"As a special birthday present for Alexander, the cast of his new musical, *Jazz It Up!* are going to perform a number from the show just for him!" the musician explained.

The guests broke into applause and cheers, and Alexander Willow looked surprised but very pleased.

"Oh, this is going to be a disaster without Jessica's magic ribbon!" Rachel said anxiously, as the dancers ran onto the stage to more applause. They looked very stylish. The women were dressed in short sequinned skirts and waistcoats while the men wore black trousers, white shirts and silk scarves knotted around their necks. They all had sparkling top hats on their heads.

Jessica was looking very sad.

"This would be a *fabulous* performance if only the Jazz Ribbon was in its proper place on my wand!" she sighed.

The jazz band struck up an upbeat tune as the dancers quickly took their places. They began to shimmy across the stage, throwing their arms up into the air in sequence, and singing,
Jazz it up!
Join us tonight and
Jazz it up!

"I can't watch," Rachel groaned, covering her eyes with her hands.

Kirsty knew exactly how Rachel felt, but she forced herself to keep looking. The men and women had separated into two groups, still singing along to the music as they began to dance.

"Those are fantastic fan kicks," Jessica murmured approvingly as the women high-kicked their way across the stage.

"And those ball changes and hip rolls are right in time with the music."

Kirsty watched curiously as the male dancers performed the splits in mid-air and the women shimmied around them. They were all dancing really well, and nothing had gone wrong yet.

"Rachel," Kirsty nudged her friend, "it's OK. The performance is going brilliantly!"

"Oh!" Rachel peeked through her fingers and then beamed at Kirsty. "But that means…"

"That my ribbon must be very close by!" Jessica chimed in excitedly.

Kirsty nodded, scanning the stage for a goblin or the magic ribbon. At first she couldn't see anything out of the ordinary, but suddenly her gaze was drawn to one of the dancers at the back. He was smaller than the others and, rather strangely, his silk scarf was

tied around his face instead of around his neck. He seemed to be the best dancer on the stage. "Look!" Kirsty said, pointing him out to Rachel and Jessica as the dancers did a final spin. "That dancer's a bit odd, isn't he?"

Jessica narrowed her eyes suspiciously.

The dancers were now sweeping off their top hats and passing them down the line to the person behind them, as they moved across the stage, but the smallest dancer refused to take his hat off, much to the annoyance of the girl behind him.

At that moment, Kirsty and Rachel both noticed that, unlike the others, the smallest dancer had a pink silk ribbon tied around his top hat.

"I recognise that ribbon!" Jessica announced, her voice trembling with excitement. "That dancer is a goblin in disguise – and he's got my magic Jazz Ribbon!"

Goblin Takes a Bow

"That explains why he was dancing so well, and the others, too!" Rachel exclaimed as the music finished and the dancers took their bows to loud applause.

"Let's follow the dancers as they come offstage, and try to get the ribbon back," Kirsty suggested.

The audience was still applauding so the dancers took a second bow.

"They were brilliant, weren't they?" said a woman at a table near Rachel and Kirsty. "I can't wait to see the show!"

"And wasn't that young boy at the back excellent?" her friend remarked.

"Luckily, nobody realises he was a goblin," Rachel whispered to Kirsty, looking relieved.

"We'd better hurry backstage,"
Kirsty replied. "We might get a chance
to grab the ribbon as the goblin
comes offstage."

Jessica quickly ducked out of sight
behind Kirsty's hair and
the two girls went
backstage. There
they hid quickly
behind a rack
of costumes
near the wings
and watched
the dancers
filing offstage.

The goblin was
last in the line. But
instead of following the other
dancers, he hurried to the front of the

stage and took another bow on his own, carefully holding the top hat on his head. The audience laughed and continued to clap. The goblin

immediately made another sweeping bow, still holding onto the top hat. This time he bent over so low that the hat was almost touching the ground. "He's enjoying himself too much to leave the stage!" Kirsty laughed as the goblin waved graciously at the audience and took yet another bow.

The girls watched in amusement as the saxophone player went over to the goblin and took his arm.

The goblin pulled himself free, skipped over to the side of the stage and bowed again. The saxophone player frowned and hurried after the goblin who managed to dodge around him and run to the *other* side of the stage. The audience was now in fits of laughter.

"They think it's all part of the show!" Rachel whispered.

At last the saxophone player managed to grab the goblin's arm and march him away.

"Remember that the goblin has the freezing power Jack Frost gave him," Jessica reminded Rachel and Kirsty. "So don't get too close to him."

The girls peeped cautiously round the rack of costumes as the goblin finally came offstage. He was humming to himself in a very satisfied way, but as he skipped along happily, he suddenly stopped. Then he pulled his silk scarf away from his face slightly, to reveal a long, green pointy nose. In fact it was the longest, pointiest goblin nose Rachel had ever seen.

She glanced at Kirsty and could tell that her friend was thinking exactly the same thing. None of the goblins had *small* noses, but this one was huge!

The goblin sniffed the air cautiously. Then he sniffed again, so hard that Rachel could see his nostrils quivering. To her horror, he spun round and walked towards the rack of costumes.

"I think the goblin's sniffed us out!" Rachel whispered urgently to Kirsty and Jessica. "He's coming straight towards us!"

Kitchen Chaos

"We've got to do something!" Kirsty whispered.

"I'll turn you into fairies right now!" Jessica said quickly, "And then we'll be able to fly away if the goblin spots us."

She waved her wand and deep pink sparkles floated down around Rachel and Kirsty, shrinking them right where

41

they stood. Gauzy, glimmering fairy

wings appeared on their backs, and the two girls smiled with delight. They'd been fairies many times before, but it was *always* so much fun.

"Now stay as still as you can!" Jessica breathed softly.

All three of them held their breath as they waited for the goblin to pull the rack of costumes aside and find them. But nothing happened. Puzzled, Rachel, Kirsty and Jessica peeped out again, just in time to see the goblin disappearing through the exit just in front of their hiding place.

"He's going outside," Rachel whispered with a sigh of relief.

"We'd better follow him!" said Jessica.

But as they zoomed after the goblin, they heard the band strike up another melody.

"I think the dancing's starting," Kirsty pointed out.

"Then we *must* get the ribbon back or it will be a disaster!" Jessica said firmly. "After that goblin, girls!"

Jessica and the girls flew out of the exit after the goblin. He was hurrying across the garden towards the manor house.

43

The three friends followed him into the house, but then he stopped, pulled down his scarf and sniffed the air again, before racing off down a long, twisting corridor.

"He can smell *something*!" Jessica whispered, as they flew after him. "But what?"

Ahead of them, the goblin had stopped in an open doorway. He was now sniffing the air very hard, with a look of delight on his face.

"I can smell it too, now. It's

freshly-baked cakes," Kirsty said. "We must be near the kitchen."

Jessica and the girls flew down the corridor and hovered just behind the goblin's head. He didn't notice them because he was peering eagerly into the kitchen where a cook, wearing a white apron, was taking a tray of delicious-looking chocolate brownies out of the oven. She put it down on the kitchen counter and reached into the oven for a second tray.

Immediately the goblin
tiptoed into the kitchen. As
Jessica, Rachel and
Kirsty watched, he
reached up and
stole one of the
freshly-baked
brownies. But he
dropped it almost
immediately
with a
loud squeal.

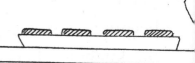

"Ow!" he yelped,
dancing up and
down and blowing
on his fingers.
"It's hot!"

The cook whipped
round and frowned at him.

"Well, it serves you right for trying to take a brownie without permission!" she said, putting down the second tray. "Let me check your hand to make sure it isn't burnt."

"Don't want to," the goblin muttered rudely, putting both hands behind his back.

"Don't be silly!" the cook scolded. As the goblin sulkily held out his hand, Jessica glanced at Rachel and Kirsty in alarm.

"What is she going to think when she sees the goblin has *green* hands?" she whispered. Rachel and Kirsty watched anxiously as the cook stared at the goblin's fingers. "Why are your hands so dirty and green?" the cook said, frowning. "Have you been rolling around on the grass?"

The goblin shrugged and didn't reply, sticking his bottom lip out sullenly.

"Wash your hands and then you can have a brownie," the cook instructed him.

"I don't want to wash my hands!" the goblin said, his face breaking into a sly smile. "But I do want to freeze YOU!"

And he jumped forward, touched the cook and shouted, *"Freeze!"*

Instantly the cook was frozen solid and Jessica, Rachel and Kirsty gasped in horror. The goblin gleefully began stuffing himself with brownies.

"The poor cook!" Jessica sighed. "Isn't it lucky that the goblin's magic doesn't last long? The freezing spell will wear off soon and at least the poor lady won't remember being frozen."

"This could be our chance to grab the ribbon," Kirsty pointed out. "The goblin's busy stuffing himself with brownies!"

"You're right," Jessica whispered. "I'll try to use my magic to untie the ribbon from the hat."

Rachel and Kirsty nodded, and flew over to hover above the goblin. Jessica waved her wand and a shower of deep pink sparkles surrounded the goblin's top hat.

Immediately the ribbon began to untie itself.

Their hearts pounding, Kirsty and Rachel flew down to grab the Jazz Ribbon.

"I wonder if there are any more brownies in the oven," the goblin muttered greedily. He turned round to look and immediately spotted Rachel and Kirsty reaching towards his top hat.

"*Freeze!*" the goblin yelled, leaping into the air to touch them.

Making a Splash

"Eek!" Kirsty squeaked, darting to her left as Rachel dodged to the right. Both girls managed to avoid the goblin's outstretched fingers, but he climbed onto a stool and then onto the kitchen counter in an effort to reach them.

"Let's get out of here!" Jessica called, whizzing over to the door. Rachel and

Kirsty were quick to follow. As they
shot out of the door, they glanced back
to see the goblin firmly re-tying the
ribbon to his hat. Then he jumped
down from the counter and dashed
after them.

"Now *he's* chasing *us!*" Rachel cried
as they flew off down the corridor with
the goblin in hot pursuit.

Jessica led the way out of the house. "Girls, we *must* keep away from the goblin or he'll freeze us!" she called anxiously as they sped across the garden. "But somehow I *have* to get my ribbon back!"

Kirsty looked round and saw the goblin charging out of the house towards them, holding onto his top hat.

"Here he comes!" she said.

Meanwhile, Rachel was staring at the swimming pool ahead of them. And, suddenly, an idea popped into her head.

"Quick, Jessica, can you make Kirsty and me human-sized again?" Rachel asked urgently. "I think there's a way we can stop the goblin *and* get the ribbon back!"

Jessica nodded, raised her wand and showered the girls with sparkles. Instantly Rachel and Kirsty shot up to their normal size again.

"I'm not scared of you!" the goblin yelled, still rushing towards them.

"I can freeze you *whatever* size you
are, ha ha!"

"Come on, Kirsty!" Rachel grabbed
her friend's hand and pulled her over
to the side of the pool while Jessica
hovered above them. "We need to jump
out of the way when I count to three!"

The goblin was careering down the
path towards the girls.

"One," Rachel whispered.

The goblin grinned gleefully as he got closer. "You can't escape me now!" he gloated.

"Two," Rachel murmured. Then, as the goblin leapt towards the girls, shouting *"Freeze!"* Rachel yelled, "THREE!"

Kirsty jumped one way and Rachel jumped the other, but the goblin was going so fast he couldn't stop.

He raced on, right to the edge of the pool. For a second he teetered there, on the brink, a look of horror on his face. But then he overbalanced and hit the water with a loud *splash.*

Jessica Jazzes Things Up

"Help!" the goblin spluttered, thrashing around in the pool.

Jessica immediately flew down and sent a stream of sparkling, dark-pink fairy dust towards his top hat. Once again the magic ribbon untied itself.

"Grab hold of one end," Jessica told the goblin. And then, with a second

swirl of sparkles, she sent the other end
of the ribbon snaking through the air
towards Rachel and Kirsty. The girls
grabbed hold of it and towed the
goblin over to the steps
at the side of
the pool. He
clambered out,
grumbling and
shivering, and
still clutching his
end of the ribbon.

"This ribbon doesn't
belong to you," Rachel told him, as she
and Kirsty clung on to *their* end just as
firmly. "You'd better give it back!"

The goblin poked his tongue out.
"Shan't!" he retorted, still shaking
with cold.

Jessica flew down to join them. "You look cold," she said to the goblin. "How about if I make you warm and dry with my magic?"

"Ooh, yes!" the goblin said eagerly.

"Well, if I do, then I want my ribbon in return!" Jessica said firmly, raising her wand and looking enquiringly at the goblin. "What do you say?"

The goblin frowned. "But I *like* the ribbon," he grumbled. "And Jack Frost told me to keep it!"

"Oh, but think how nice it would be to be lovely and warm and dry!" Kirsty put in. She winked at Rachel and Jessica.

They all knew that goblins *hated* being wet!

The goblin looked undecided. "It *would* be nice," he agreed slowly.

"And we won't tell Jack Frost you've given the ribbon to us," Rachel promised.

The goblin glanced at Jessica. "But can you make me really, *really* warm?" he asked.

Jessica nodded.

"OK, you can keep the ribbon then!" the goblin declared, dropping his end of the Jazz Ribbon immediately. Rachel and Kirsty glanced at each other in

64

delight and Jessica tapped the goblin's top hat with her wand. As sparkling pink fairy dust whirled down around him, drying him off, the goblin's face broke into a big smile.

"Ooh, I'm warm all over!" he sighed blissfully. "My toes are toasty!"

And then he skipped off happily across the garden.

Rachel and Kirsty let go of the magic ribbon and it floated over to Jessica. As it did so, it shrank down to its Fairyland size. Then it reattached itself to her wand, glowing an even deeper, more vivid pink as it did so.

"Hurrah!" Jessica cried, stroking her ribbon as it waved gently in the evening breeze. "We did it, girls! Thank you a million times for all your help!"

Rachel and Kirsty grinned at each other.

"The party should go well now," Kirsty pointed out.

"Of course it will!" Jessica declared. "You go and enjoy yourselves – you deserve it!" And with a wink, the little fairy disappeared in a cloud of pink fairy magic.

The girls hurried back to the marquee, but when they went inside, they were both dismayed by the scene in front of them: the music had stopped, some of the tables and chairs had been knocked over, and a couple of people were hobbling off the dance floor, shaking their heads and looking very glum.

"Oh, no!" Rachel groaned. "It looks like the dancing's been a catastrophe!"

"I think they must have bumped into each other!" Kirsty added, pointing at two people who were sitting on the floor, looking very dazed and rubbing their heads.

Suddenly, Rachel spied Mrs Tate sitting on one chair with her leg

propped up on another. The two
girls quickly ran over to her.

"Hello, girls," said Mrs Tate, trying
to smile. "I twisted my ankle when
I was dancing. It's very sore."

"Oh, poor you!" Kirsty cried.

Suddenly, a pink sparkle caught
Rachel's eye. She nudged Kirsty and they
glanced up to see Jessica
sitting on one of
the gold stars
hanging from
the ceiling.
Jessica was
waving her wand
to and fro, and
suddenly the band
began to play again. People looked at
each other hesitantly, wondering whether

to dance again or not.

"Oh!" Mrs Tate exclaimed, looking surprised. "Do you know, I think my ankle's stopped hurting?" She swung her leg down to the floor and stood up carefully. "Yes, it feels absolutely fine now! Shall we go and dance?"

"Oh, yes!" Rachel and Kirsty chorused, exchanging a smile as they realised that Jessica's fairy magic must

have healed Mrs Tate's ankle.

The two girls and Kirsty's mum moved onto the dance floor. People watched rather nervously at first, but when they realised that nothing was going wrong, they began to join in.

As more people crowded onto the dance floor, Rachel and Kirsty glanced up to see Jessica smiling down at them. Then, with a dainty wave, the little fairy vanished in a swirl of sparkling magic.

"The party's going brilliantly now!" Rachel said.

Kirsty nodded. "And so is the dancing," she said happily. Then she added in a whisper, "Thanks, Jessica!"

**Now Rachel and Kirsty
must help...**

Saskia the Salsa Fairy

Read on for a sneak peek...

"See you later, Mum," Kirsty Tate said,
as she and her best friend, Rachel
Walker, got ready to leave the house.

"Four o'clock, in front of the Village
Hall," Mrs Tate reminded the girls.
"I should have finished my work by
then. I'm sure you'll have a great time at
the fiesta. I can't wait to see all the
dancing and costumes. Now, girls,
promise me that you'll stick together; it's
going to be very busy."

"We will," Kirsty promised. Then, as
she and Rachel set off down the road,

she added to Rachel, "Of course we'll stick together. Isn't that when we have all our best adventures?"

Rachel grinned. "I hope we have another one today," she replied.

Rachel was staying with Kirsty's family for half-term and the girls were having a very exciting week. A *fairy* exciting week, in fact, because they were helping the Dance Fairies find their missing magical ribbons. The Dance Ribbons helped dancers perform their best throughout Fairyland as well as all around the human world, but Jack Frost, a bad fairy, had stolen the ribbons in order to make sure his goblin servants would dance well at his parties. The Fairy King and Queen had heard about the stolen ribbons, and they'd been to

Jack Frost's ice castle to get them back.

Unfortunately, Jack Frost had seen them coming, and he had immediately cast a spell to hurl all the ribbons into the human world, with a goblin to guard each one.

While the ribbons were missing, dancing was going wrong in Fairyland and all over the world. Luckily, Kirsty and Rachel had helped the fairies find the Ballet, Disco, Rock 'n' Roll, Tap Dance, and Jazz Ribbons, and these ribbons were now safely back with their rightful fairy owners. There were still two dance ribbons out there somewhere, though, and the girls were keen to track them down.

"The Salsa Ribbon is still lost," Kirsty said, as they walked towards the centre of the village, where the fiesta was taking place. "I wonder if the goblin guarding it will be attracted to the salsa music and turn up at the fiesta today. I hope so."

Rachel was nodding. "If he's anything like the others, having the ribbon will just make him want to dance, dance, dance," she agreed. "And with all that salsa music playing, I bet he won't be able to resist."

The girls had been surprised at first to see that the goblins who were guarding the dance ribbons could dance really well. In fact, dancing seemed to be the only thing they wanted to do, and any time they heard a tune connected with their particular dance ribbon, they seemed drawn to the music. The fairies had explained to the girls that it was actually the ribbons' magic that made the goblins dance so well. The power of the dance ribbons was so strong that they made anybody nearby dance wonderfully well – even clumsy goblins!

Kirsty glanced around. "Well, I hope the goblin with the Salsa Ribbon does turn up," she said quietly. "That way we might be able to get the ribbon away from him and safely back to Saskia the Salsa Fairy," she added. "If we don't, the salsa dancing is going to be ruined today!"

Read Saskia the Salsa Fairy to find out what adventures are in store for Kirsty and Rachel!

Meet the
Dance Fairies

Jack Frost has stolen the Dance Fairies' magic ribbons! Kirsty and Rachel must get them back, or dance everywhere will be ruined.

www.rainbowmagicbooks.co.uk

Calling all parents, carers and teachers!
The Rainbow Magic fairies are here to help
your child enter the magical world of reading.
Whatever reading stage they are at, there's
a Rainbow Magic book for everyone!
Here is Lydia the Reading Fairy's guide to
supporting your child's journey at all levels.

Starting Out

Our Rainbow Magic Beginner Readers are perfect for first-time readers who are just beginning to develop reading skills and confidence. Approved by teachers, they contain a full range of educational levelling, as well as lively full-colour illustrations.

Developing Readers

Rainbow Magic Early Readers contain longer stories and wider vocabulary for building stamina and growing confidence. These are adaptations of our most popular Rainbow Magic stories, specially developed for younger readers in conjunction with an Early Years reading consultant, with full-colour illustrations.

Going Solo

The Rainbow Magic chapter books – a mixture of series and one-off specials – contain accessible writing to encourage your child to venture into reading independently. These highly collectible and much-loved magical stories inspire a love of reading to last a lifetime.

www.rainbowmagicbooks.co.uk

"Rainbow Magic got my daughter reading chapter books. Great sparkly covers, cute fairies and traditional stories full of magic that she found impossible to put down" – Mother of Edie (6 years)

"Florence LOVES the Rainbow Magic books. She really enjoys reading now" – Mother of Florence (6 years)

The Rainbow Magic Reading Challenge

Well done, fairy friend – you have completed the book!
This book was worth 5 points.

See how far you have climbed on the
Reading Rainbow opposite.

The more books you read, the more points you will get,
and the closer you will be to becoming a Fairy Princess!

How to get your Reading Rainbow
1. Cut out the coin below
2. Go to the Rainbow Magic website
3. Download and print out your poster
4. Add your coin and climb up the Reading Rainbow!

There's all this and lots more at
www.rainbowmagicbooks.co.uk

You'll find activities, competitions, stories, a special
newsletter and complete profiles of all the
Rainbow Magic fairies. Find a fairy with your name!